For Payton and Callie

ONCE UPON a time, there was a little unicorn named Agnes.

She lived in the woods with not too many people to talk to because she was, well, different.

The other unicorns would tease her because she didn't sparkle like they did. Not only did she not sparkle, but she was, in fact, of a gray color.

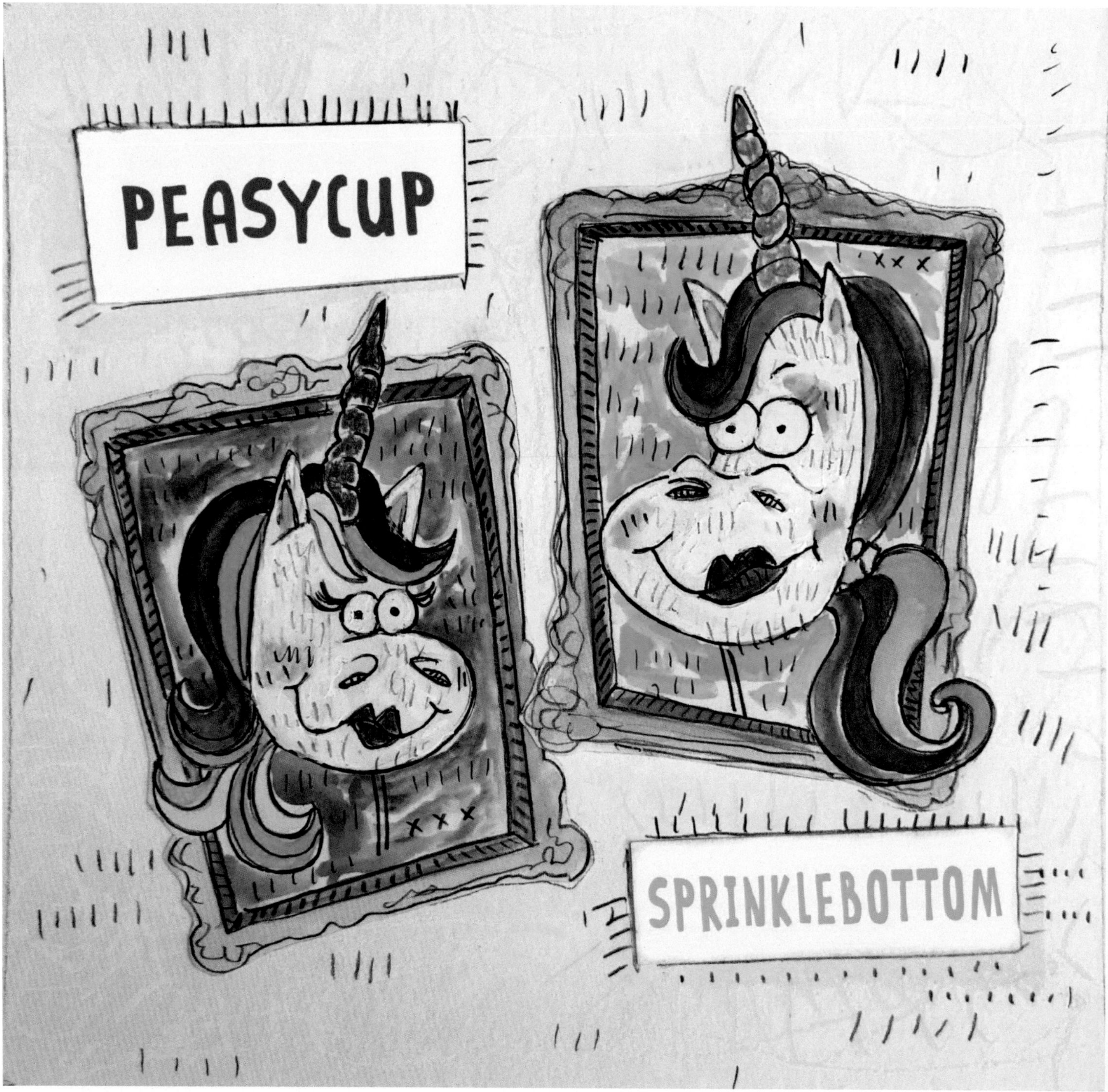
PEASYCUP
SPRINKLEBOTTOM

The other unicorns would often tease her, and the worst of these were named SprinkleBottom and Peaseycup.

Both SprinkleBottom and Peaseycup would taunt her about her color, how her horn didn't shape up like theirs did, and how she couldn't make rainbows when she galloped.

Day by day, in an attempt to fit in with the other unicorns, she
Would gallop around the woods trying to make rainbows
happen.

She galloped one time, and made a dishwasher. She tried again,
and made broccoli. She galloped a third time, and made some
really neat beach balls, but she could never come up with a
rainbow, no matter how hard she tried.

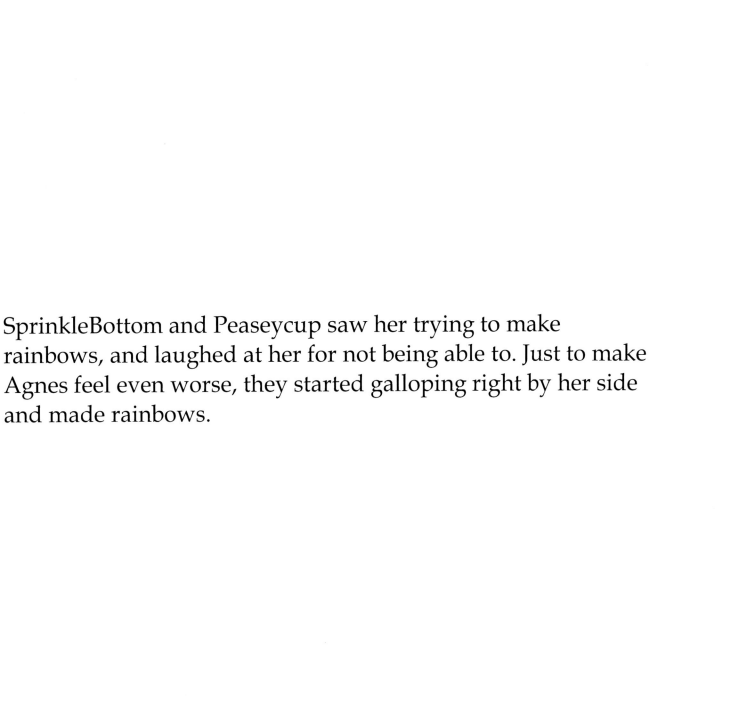

SprinkleBottom and Peaseycup saw her trying to make rainbows, and laughed at her for not being able to. Just to make Agnes feel even worse, they started galloping right by her side and made rainbows.

They would say "Agnes, why can't you do this? Every other unicorn can do this, and we make kids happy because we can! You'll never be a unicorn because you can't make any kid happy! You just make things that no one likes when YOU gallop! You're NOT A REAL UNICORN! YOU'RE JUST A HORSE WITH A HORN!"

Agnes was sad when SprinkleBottom and Peaseycup would tease her, and she felt that she would never fit in. She would watch the other unicorns frolic and make rainbows left and right. She would watch the other unicorns enjoying cotton candy and peppermint sticks during lunch, and she would just eat grass instead.

This, of course, made the other unicorns tease her even more. They would yell at her: "YOU'RE EATING GRASS?!? THAT'S SO GROSS! YOU'RE SO WEIRD! WHY CAN'T YOU BE NORMAL LIKE US? YOU'RE SO AVERAGE!" and they would throw cotton candy and peppermint sticks at her for being so different.

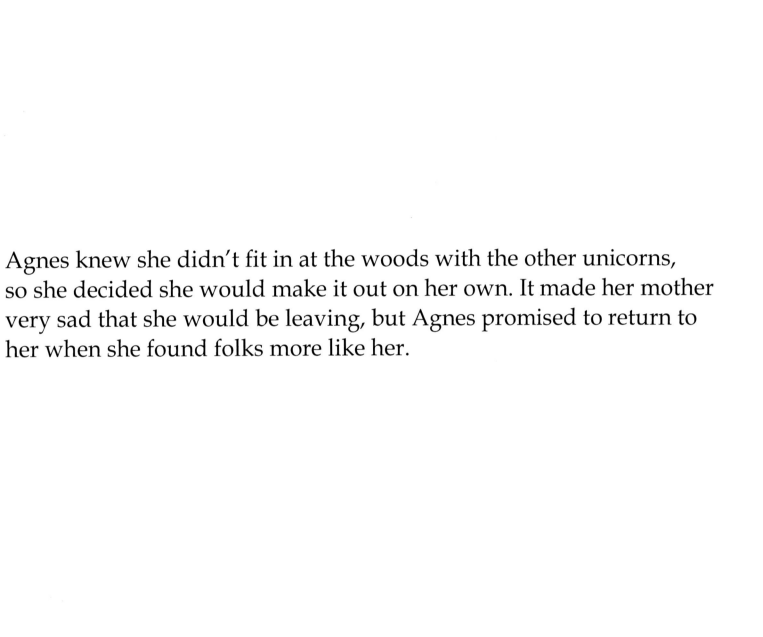

Agnes knew she didn't fit in at the woods with the other unicorns, so she decided she would make it out on her own. It made her mother very sad that she would be leaving, but Agnes promised to return to her when she found folks more like her.

Her mother told her that she loved her very much, but she understood how mean the other unicorns were to her. Agnes bumped her horn against her mother's horn and set out to find her way. She galloped away, leaving behind her a trail of pennies, a couple of records, and three pieces of licorice candy.

Agnes had never been outside of the woods in her life, and it was a little scary at first. There were buildings and cars all over the place, and everyone was in a hurry. No one even seemed to notice that she was a unicorn at all because they were too busy looking at their screens of their phones. One man looked up and told Agnes that horses don't belong in the city, and that she needed to be back on the farm where she belonged.

Agnes had no idea what a farm was, so she kept going through the city.

The buildings were so big, and everyone was moving so fast that she had to find a place to rest. She came across a building that had a lot of grass around it, and she stopped there to eat. After eating, she looked up and saw a fence around the back of the building she was at with human children playing inside a fence.

The children were playing a game, and this made Agnes very happy to watch. One child would roll a red ball on the ground, and another child would kick it as hard as he or she could and then run in a circle.

One child waited for the ball to be rolled to her, and she kicked it so hard that it went way, way up in the air, and it seemed to be heading towards where Agnes was.

Agnes got excited and galloped towards the ball heading towards her. The ball came right to where her horn was and then—POP!

Agnes stood in the grass, confused. This thing that was once a ball was now a flappy piece of rubber that was stuck on her horn. What was this? Had she done something good? Did she win?
The children ran up to where she was on the fence. Agnes stood there, not knowing what to do with this piece of red, flappy rubber that was still stuck to her horn.

One boy yelled: "YOU RUINED OUR KICKBALL GAME! NOW WE HAVE TO GO BACK INSIDE TO SCHOOL AND GO LEARN! GIVE US OUR BALL BACK, YOU DUMB UNICORN!"

Agnes approached the fence, and the boy ripped the flappy rubber thing off Agnes' horn. One girl stuck around after all the other children went back inside, and told Agnes that it was okay, and she thought she was a pretty unicorn. She then found a ball that was left on the playground and threw it over the fence to Agnes.

Agnes liked the ball, but she didn't know what to do with it. She jumped around the ball and snorted at it, but the ball refused to move. Agnes sighed, and gently pushed the ball with her hoof, and the ball moved slightly.

Agnes pushed the ball again with her horn, only this time a little harder. The ball moved even more this time. Every time the ball moved a little further, she would run after the ball and push it with her hoof even more.

Agnes tried to make it back to her woods to show her mother what she could do, but she got lost on the way, and ended up in a different part than where she lived. She came across some fairies that were living there, and while they weren't mean to her, they also didn't have much to do with her. Agnes kept kicking her ball around, and when she looked up, there was a fairy sitting on a log and watching her.

Agnes looked at the fairy and said "why are you sitting on that log and watching me kick my ball around?" "Why aren't you out flying with the other fairies?"

The fairy looked embarrassed for a second and replied: "I can't fly. I mean, I CAN, but I only have one wing. Every time I try to fly, I end up just flying in circles, so I just walk. Why are YOU just kicking a ball around? Shouldn't you be galloping rainbows and eating cotton candy and peppermint sticks?"

Agnes shook her horn a little bit and replied: "whenever I try to gallop, a bunch of useless stuff comes out of it. And I don't like cotton candy, nor do I like peppermint sticks. I really like kicking this ball around, and I like playing kickball.
What's your name?"

The fairy said: "I'm Ralph. Ralph the fairy. I think that I would like to play kickball with you. I don't really know how to play, but much like you, I don't quite fit in with the other fairies here either. I might even be pretty good at kickball. Can I come with you and play kickball? What do they call you? Is it a typical unicorn name? SpizzleSpazzle? Miss SparkleDazzle?"

"Agnes", said Agnes. "Just plain old Agnes." "Ah," said Ralph. "Well, I'm just plain old Ralph." "Perhaps we could be plain and old together? And play kickball?"

"Of course", said Agnes. Ralph tried to fly over to where Agnes was, but couldn't get too close to her, as he just kept spinning in a circle with his one wing. Agnes kicked the ball towards him, and in the middle of one of his spins, Ralph kicked the ball deeper into the woods. Ralph stopped spinning and sat back down on the log. "I'm sorry, Agnes. I didn't know how fast I was spinning." "It's okay, Ralph", said Agnes. "Hop on my back, and we'll go and find the ball and we can play some more."

It took Ralph a few times to get on Agnes' back, but eventually, he made it on there.

As the new found friends went deeper into the woods, they came across a clearing where a bunch of human men were standing around a fire. Ralph was a little nervous, but Agnes assured him that everything was going to be okay. As they walked towards the fire, one of the men said: "whoa, whoa, whoa. Both you and your one winged fairy need to back up. This fire is for werewolves only, and when the moon finally comes out, we're going to turn into wolves and go around the woods scaring people and eating everything we see."

Agnes replied: "well, my friend Ralph and I are just looking for my ball. We don't want to be eaten up, and we're trying to find my ball so we can play kickball." The men started to howl and laugh at the same time. One of the men said: "UNICORNS DON'T PLAY KICKBALL! THEY FROLIC AND MAKE RAINBOWS AND EAT COTTON CANDY AND PEPPERMINT STICKS! AND FAIRIES HAVE TWO WINGS, NOT ONE! GUYS, THESE TWO SHOULD HANG OUT WITH GARY!"

Agnes and Ralph looked around, and saw a man standing away from everyone else. He looked like all the other men standing around the fire, but just like Agnes and Ralph, he didn't fit in with the other werewolves. Agnes and Ralph walked up to the lonely man. Ralph said: "Agnes, don't do this! He's just another werewolf, and when the moon comes out, he's going to eat us up!"

Agnes ignored the warning, and headed towards the man. "Are you Gary?" she asked him. The man sadly nodded, and said "I'm not a very good werewolf. Whenever the moon is full, all the other guys want to go out and eat everything they can find. When I turn into a wolf, all I really want to do is go and find a nice salad bar and eat salad. The other guys all think I'm weird, and I think I'll never fit in. I've found this ball, and I've been playing with it to pass the time until the moon comes out and I head to the salad bar."

Agnes' eyes lit up. "That's our ball! Ralph and I were going to go and practice so we could become good at kickball and play a game with the other children at the school I found!" Gary asked: "do you mind if I come and play kickball with you? Clearly I'm not good at being a werewolf, but I used to be really good at kickball when I was a little boy. I could teach you both how to play. Would you mind?"

"Not at all!" said Agnes. And the two kickball players became three.

It was hard playing kickball at first. Agnes came close to popping the ball a lot, Ralph just flew in circles, and every thirtieth day, Gary couldn't make it to practice as he was at the salad bar. Gary was smart, however, and figured out that Agnes wouldn't pop the ball if something was over her horn. He had an old lampshade at his house, and it protected Agnes from popping the only ball they had. Gary even made a small wing out of popsicle sticks and fixed it to Ralph's back so he could fly straight. The three friends practiced day and night and became pretty good at kickball.

One day, Agnes, Ralph, and Gary went out to the school where the kids were playing. One little boy yelled: "OH, GREAT. THAT DUMB UNICORN THAT POPPED OUR BALL IS BACK, AND SHE BROUGHT HER LOSER FRIENDS WITH HER!" Agnes snorted, but Gary petted her head and said back to the boy: "yeah, but this is my team. And we're pretty good. How about us three against your entire class?"

All the kids roared with laughter. A unicorn with a lampshade on her horn, a fairy with a wing made out of popsicle sticks, and a middle aged guy? NO WAY were they going to beat Miss Tolverson's third grade class. The kids agreed, and the three took the field. Agnes played outfield, Ralph was the entire infield, and Gary was the pitcher. After one inning, Miss Tolverson's class did not score one run. If they kicked it into the infield, Ralph was so fast that he stopped their shots, and tagged them out. If they kicked it to the outfield, Agnes used the lampshade to head butt the ball back to Gary or Ralph.

When it was their time to kick the ball, Ralph took off his popsicle wing and kicked it out of the park. Gary would find the gaps in Miss Tolverson's third grade class, and Agnes would leave obstacles of packs of bubble gum, yo-yos, and chicken biscuits when she would gallop along the bases. Miss Tolverson's class did not score one run the entire game, and Agnes' team scored about five hundred runs.

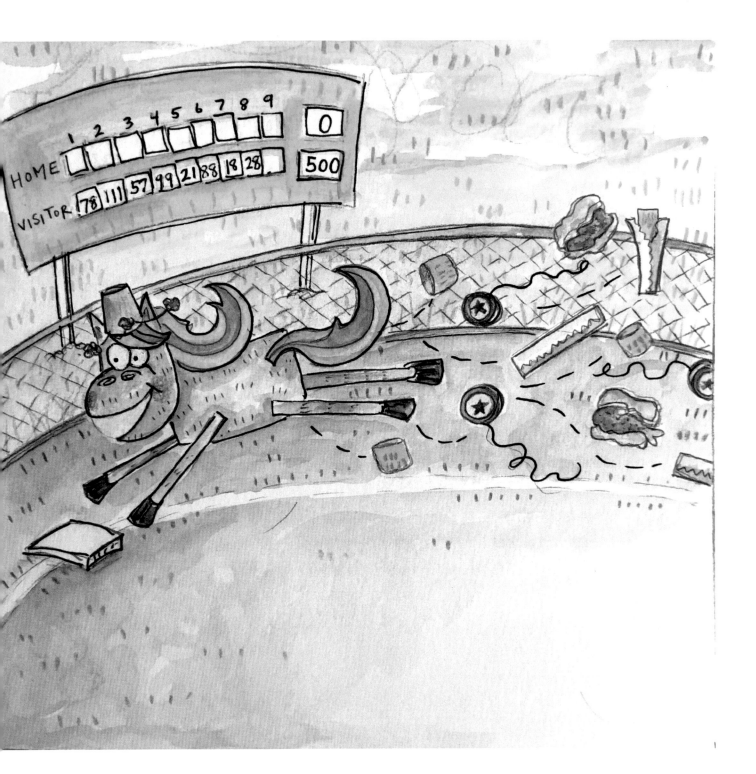

The three celebrated, and as they did, a man came up to the edge of the fence whose name was Mister Hizenplatz. He told them that he was a talent scout for a professional kickball league, and that he wanted them to join the team. Gary wanted to make sure that they didn't have any games on the thirtieth, and Mister Hizenplatz said that they would not.

The three joined the league, and travelled all around wowing everyone with their kickball skills. If people laughed at them at first, they were not laughing at the end of the game. Agnes and her friends were guests on talk shows on televisions all over the country.

But Agnes missed her mother. She wanted to go back to the woods and show all the unicorns that she WAS NOT odd, and that she was really good at kickball. She asked Mister Hizenplatz if they could go back to the woods, and Mister Hizenplatz said: "anything for one of my star players!"

So, back they went.

When Agnes first showed back up, SprinkleBottom and Peaseycup were the first ones to start teasing Agnes. They also teased Ralph and Gary as well. Agnes was sad at first, but then she told all the unicorns that while she couldn't make rainbows, she could play kickball very well. Peasycup laughed at this and said: "Agnes, don't you know that unicorns are the best at every game we play? We practically invented games! And you're hiding your horn with that foolish lampshade! You'll never be as good or as pretty as the rest of us!"

Agnes lifted her lamp-shaded head and responded: "I don't have to be. The only thing I have to be is me. And I like my lamp shade. It was given to me by my friend Gary. And Ralph is my friend too. You can say mean things, but I've got friends who don't think those things about me. They like me, and I like them. Now, do you other unicorns want to play kickball or not?"

The only thing I have to be is ME

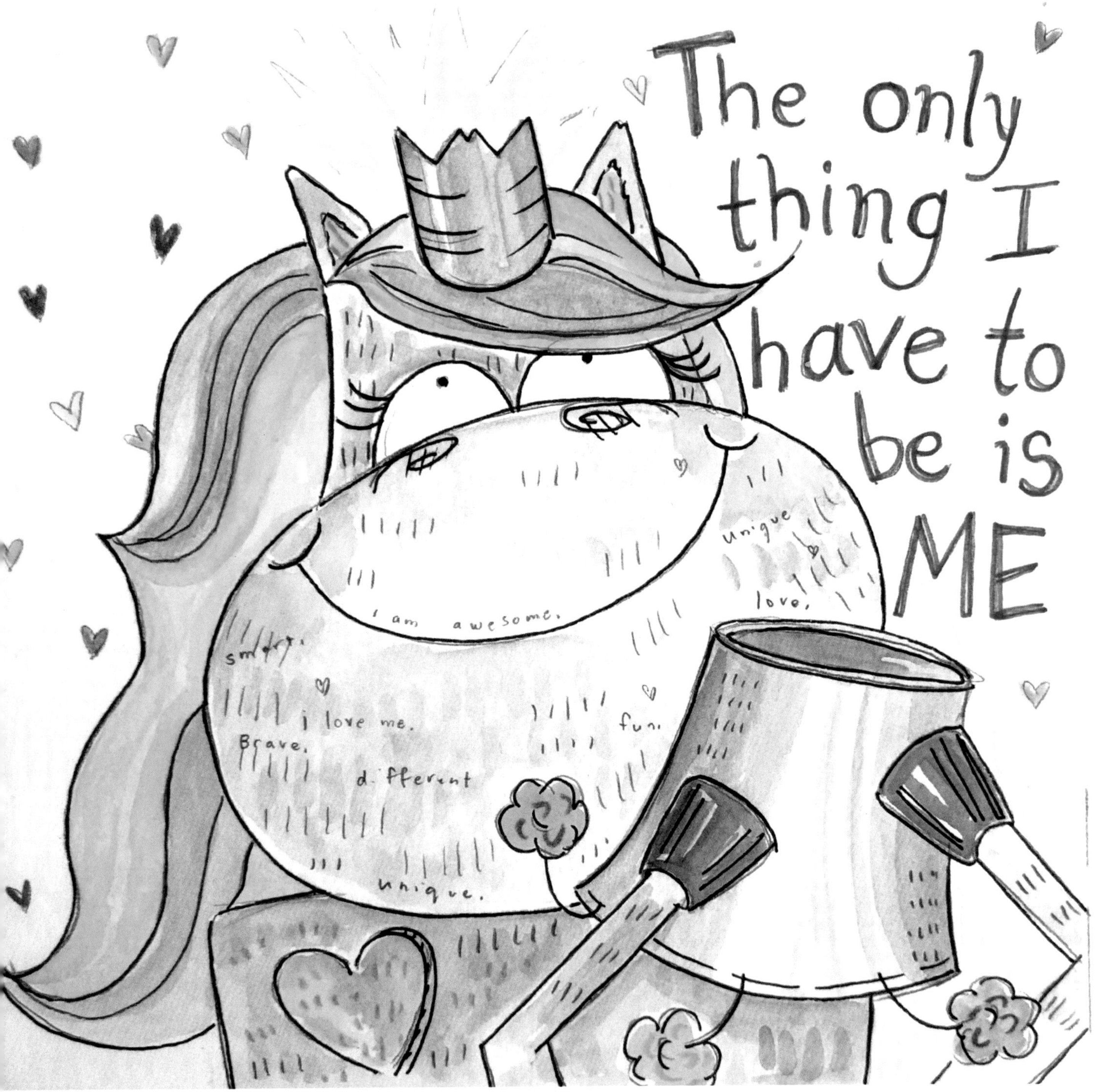

SprinkleBottom and Peaseycup accepted the challenge, and the game was on. There was no score for a long time until Agnes came to the plate. There had been so much commotion in the woods from the game that the fairies and the werewolves showed up to watch.

The fairies recognized Ralph, and the werewolves recognized Gary. They made little banners to hold up for them when the game was going on. Agnes' mother held up a little banner for Agnes. SprinkleBottom rolled the ball towards Agnes, and Agnes gave it a heavy kick.

The ball lifted into the air — WOOSH!

Agnes started to gallop towards first as fast as she could. There were old comic books, shiny nickels, and packets of seeds that would appear when her hooves hit the ground. As she rounded first, there were expired gift cards, strange action figures, and small newts.

She rounded second, and the silliness continued coming from her hoofs. There were thirty-six marshmallows, five ninjas, and three buttons from a shirt from 1986.

When she rounded third and was heading home, there was a sea of odd products flying from her hooves. Ralph and Gary were cheering her home, the fairies were cheering, the werewolves were cheering, and Agnes' mom was cheering. Peaseycup kicked the ball as hard as she could back to SprinkleBottom, and as SprinkleBottom turned to try and put Agnes out, she found herself quite trapped in the sea of random product that came out of Agnes' hooves.

Agnes touched home, and the game was over

SprinkleBottom and Peaseycup were still trapped in the sea of product, and probably would be there for some time to come.

Agnes' mom was the first one over, and they bumped horn to lampshade. The other unicorns had never seen kickball played so well, and they all ran up to congratulate Agnes, Ralph, and Gary.

And Agnes was happy. Not just because she and her friends won the game, but because she had new friends, and she went from average to awesome. She didn't need to sparkle. She didn't need to eat cotton candy. Gary could eat salad, and Ralph could be with one wing.

They were all fine just the way they were.

Made in the USA
Columbia, SC
06 November 2018